Short Stories

Short Stories

by

Charles Shelton

ISBN: 978-1-7336235-1-3

DEDICATION

I would like to dedicate this book to my wife, children, and grandchildren, who mean a great deal to me and have greatly enriched my life in so many ways.

CONTENTS

ACKNOWLEDGMENTS

I would like to give special thanks to my beautiful wife for her love and support, and for her putting up with my personal goals, along with a mixed variety of creative endeavors.

Besides my wife, I would like to thank our children and grandchildren for their patience and understanding concerning the time and efforts that were required to complete this project, but, more importantly, for making us so proud of them and their individual achievements.

In addition, I would also like to thank my brothers and sisters for the encouragement and support that they've provided throughout my life in general.

Lastly, and most of all, thanks be to God for all the wonders of his creation and the marvelous demonstrations of his love.

Story 1

FINDING THE LOST MAN

THAT LIES WITHIN – ME

I walked the lonely streets alone for many a year, searching to find the lost man that lies within—me. Not having any help, sure direction or guide, and not knowing exactly where to look, I soon became disheartened, and confused. Because no matter where and how hard I searched, I just couldn't seem to find, the lost man that lies within—me.

So I turned to living a debauched life of sin and crime. And I indulged myself in pleasures of various kinds; anything, to help ease the pain, to wipe away the blues from my heart and mind. But these vices and pursuits only made matters worse. Because I still couldn't find, the lost man that lies within—me.

One day, a certain man happened to pass my way. He had gray hair and a beard, and a timeworn face. And so I stopped him to ask for his help, hoping that he could perhaps provide direction, or shed some valuable light, on how I might find the lost man that lies within—me. I reasoned that, surely, this well seasoned old man, with the knowledge, wisdom, and experience that he has gained throughout his lifelong years, would easily be able to provide the direction I need, even if it be just a small crumb or a kernel of truth that would be useful to me to find, the lost man that lies within—me.

After clearly explaining my dilemma, and expressing to him my desperate and urgent need, the old man, without uttering one single word, leaned forward. And he peered into my misty eyes. Then, he shrugged his shoulders, and shook his head. Afterwards, he turned around, and continued moving on ahead, down a long and twisted road, in his own fixed path. I guess he just didn't have much to say or share?

Sadly, the discouraging encounter with the old man only left me feeling more baffled, exasperated, and lost. You see, I've always had such a strong yearning, an eager desire to find that poor ole soul that I'm so desperately seeking to find, the lost man that lies within—me.

Not satisfied with the present, or settling for anything less; not wanting to live just any ole life, I continued on my steadfast and arduous journey, still hoping; still seeking to find, the lost man that lies within—me. Then, suddenly, the night turned pitch-black. And the air became bitterly cold. But I didn't have a sweater or anything, to comfort and warm my freezing soul.

After the darkness and coldness roughly set in, it became ever more soberly clear to me, just how deeply I was lost. That's when a horrible fear grabbed hold of me. And I began to further question, and even doubt, that I might find the lost man that lies within—me.

Following fear; came further frustration, anger, increasing sorrow and pain. The kind of things, all working together in unison, can torment a soul, and totally rob one of peace. And I started to lose all hope, that I would truly ever find the lost man that lies within—me.

As days and years passed by, I verbally lashed out at people that I rubbed shoulders with. Because, nobody; not a single soul, didn't seem to understand or even care, about the miserable plight that I was in. Sadly, the insensitivity of their cold hearts left me feeling lonelier, down, and depressed. And I began to despise them for this, and avoid them. Because they made the hurt I feel a whole lot worse.

Later, one day, as I was walked along the city streets, with my head hanging low, and in sober thought; just out of the blue, I looked up, and when I did, I caught sight of my reflection in a sheet of glass. It appeared in a hazy storefront window as I passed. But the image I saw didn't seem to match the vision of the man in my head, the one I was hoping to find; the lost man that lies within—me. Perhaps the tears in my eyes got in the way, and prevented me from being able to clearly see. Whatever the case, I left brokenhearted and down. However, still onward bound, and determined, to find the lost man that lies within—me.

As I continued to travel through life, I looked for landmarks, signs, and clues; anything, that might help to lead me to, the lost man that lies within—me. But the sights and sounds that I was seeing and hearing, were not inherently familiar to my soul. They only left me feeling more puzzled, disoriented, and lost.

Often, in life, there are many obstacles that get in one's way, when they are pursuing a vision, a goal, or a dream — like the things that were impeding my efforts to find the lost man that lies within—me.

Finally, one day, when I was about to give up on my search; completely concede defeat; throw in the towel; suddenly, the heavy grey clouds that forever loom above my head, broke open in the sky. And a thick callus fell from my eyes. Afterwards, the sun came out, and it began to shine ever so bright. So brightly, that it illuminated my heart, mind, and darkened soul. Then, it happened. At a time that I would have least expected it to occur. He appeared! The man I thought was forever lost within—me. The person I've always longed to see and know. He miraculously arrived and stood before my very soul! The experience was so touching and moving that I could barely believe my eyes! Now, for the very first time in my life, my face began to light up and glow. And, immediately, I broke down and started to cry. Because of the sheer joy I was feeling inside. For he took away all the anger, frustration, and loneliness I use to feel. And the pain I felt for so long; finally began to heal. No, this was no imaginative dream that I was having; it was all so genuine, and ever so real!

Now, because of him, the man within—me, who was once lost, but now is found, I'm seeing life anew and in a completely different way. Because the tormented and lost soul that I became in the past, has finally been set free at last. For upon his arrival, he bestowed upon me a very special gift; something that not too many people in life come to possess; an important element that's absolutely vital to one's soul; their peace, happiness, and wellbeing, and that is, a love of self.

The strange thing is, now, I've also come to have love for other people too. But this is a good thing, a true blessing. Because this new outlook, along with finding the lost man that lies within—me, helps me to keep anger in control and pain at bay. And it prevents the troublesome, ugly things of my past, from resurfacing to re-plague my mind, heart, and soul, the way that they use to.

This wonderful and drastic change of mind and heart, along with the most important thing, which is, finding the man that was lost within—me; I owe, not to anything in particular that I personally did. However, I guess it does help when you start to accept people and things for the way they are. It also helps when you finally let go of your past; the things that left you bitter, angry, and scarred.

It's not that things are totally rosy now, for this is no made up fairytale, some imagined *"Cinderella Dream."* I still have to face the daily realities of life, and any challenges that come my way. But at least I've found an inner peace, joy, happiness, and contentment that I had never known and experienced before. Precious and priceless qualities, that are by far more valuable than any diamonds, gold, or material possessions that one can possess. Because the man within—me, the person who was once lost, has now been found, and he is free!

True, many years were lost in my search, looking to find the lost man that lies within—me. For through the process I've grown old and gray. But, although the journey was both long and painful, it was well worth all the time and effort spent. For it brings much joy to my heart and soul to know, that the man within—me, is no longer lost, but that he is finally here!

Now, I'm as free as a bird, that is no longer kept down, for I can now see, hear, feel, and discover many things; things that were hidden from and eluded me in the past; amazing things that are far above and beyond this world. But the most important and rewarding thing of all is, I'm now able to spend the exciting and valuable time left, with the beautiful man that lies within—Me!

Story 2

NO VACANCY HERE

I recently met some new friends. They came to me in my hour of need. You see, my whole world had fallen apart; I was down in the dumps; and my heart had begun to bleed.

One day, I awoke to a loud knocking and rapping at my door. As I lay there in bed, thoroughly agitated and annoyed, by the unexpected sound and disturbance, I yelled out: "Who is it?" But, there was no response; just a steady knocking and rapping at my door.

"Go away! Let me be! Can't you see that I am trying to sleep?" I angrily shouted. But, still no response, just a knocking and rapping at my door.

I grumbled and muttered to myself: "Who can this be, at this early hour of the day? Why don't they just go away and leave me alone to stay?"

Knock, knock, knock… rap, rap, rap… goes the annoying and

disturbing sound again.

So I forcefully and painfully pulled myself out of bed, and stumbled to the door. Then, I flung the door open, and yelled: "What do you want?"

The person on the other side of the door, dressed in a long, white overcoat, and clutching a traveling pack in his hand, respectfully and calmly said: "Hello, I'm sorry to wake you, Sir. Sorry to trouble you, indeed I am. My name is Peace. I'm just a traveler passing through, looking for a place to rest."

"I don't think I have the space? You see, this place is small, and a little cramped for room," I responded to Peace, hoping that he would just turn and leave soon.

"That's quite okay with me, Sir. I don't need much room; just a place to rest my head. Also, from the visual signs above, the way things are looking in the dark and cloudy sky, shelter from the coming storm," Peace replied.

With that being said; what could I say? So I opened up and invited Peace inside.

Later that night, as Peace and I sat together and talked, I told him my sad story, about how everything fell apart, and how it completely broke my heart.

Peace sat and listened patiently until I was done speaking. Then he reached into his travel pack and pulled out a fiddle, and he started to play and sing. He played a very charming tune, and sang with an angel's voice. It was the most beautiful and soothing thing I have ever heard! It made me feel restful, cozy, and warm. And, before you knew it, I dosed off and fell sound asleep.

The next day, once again, I awoke to a loud knock at my door. So I rose up to see who it was. It was a stranger; someone named, Love. He said: "I'm but a traveler passing through, looking for a place to stay."

"Peace is already here. I don't know if I have the room for one more soul to lay?" I replied.

"I traveled a long way, from a distance land afar. I won't take up much space. I'm just looking for shelter, before daylight turns to dark," Love, entreatingly remarked.

So I gave in and opened up and let Love inside, for he processed a true sincerely that I just could not deny.

Later, in the evening, as Love and I sat together and talked, I told him my sad story about how everything fell apart; how it broke my heart; and how bad I felt. All the while, Love sat patiently, listening till I was done speaking. Then, Love told me a story about a man he used to know. He said: "Initially, there was a man that had a very good and tender heart. But, then, in time, he had undergone some very difficult problems that caused him a lot of pain and sorrow; horrible things that brought him to his knees, and that made his heart break and bleed. As a result, the man eventually wound up moving far away, completely isolating himself from the cold and cruel world. And, unfortunately, he turned bitter and sad. For from day to day, things only got worse for him, and increasing bad."

Apparently, the man's story was so sad to relate, that it brought Love to tears! At one point, he even paused, the lump in his throat to clear.

Interestingly, the man's story that Love was relating seemed so similar to mine. It was like I was peering into a mirror and seeing myself for the very first time. Then, suddenly, bewildering things that seemed so puzzling to me in the past, started to come together and make perfect sense; as sunlight began to rise and flood into the dark shadows of my mind. And, as my vision began to clear and un-fog, I also began to hear the sound of my heart, and feel its rhythmic beat and feelings once again. And, before you knew it, I dosed off and fell into a deep and wonderful, blissful sleep.

The next day, again, I awoke to a knock at my door. When I answered, it was another stranger. His name was Joy, with the heart of a boy. He said: "I'm a traveler passing through, looking for a place to lodge."

"I don't think I have the room, since I now have Peace, and Love," I answered.

"I won't take up too much space. I just need a place to reside. So please dear Sir, if you will, please let me come inside," Joy replied.

"Alright, come on in," I finally said.

Later that night, as Joy and I sat around and talked, I told him my sad story about what had happened to me; but then, how Peace and Love came and knocked at my door, and how they both moved in. In response, Joy said: "I'm glad to hear that things for you have positively turned around. The last thing you need in life is to be lying with your face buried in the ground. You know, I think this calls for a celebration, a time to laugh and cheer!" At this, Joy quickly sprung to his feet, and started to move and dance, as his face lit up and shined with a joyful radiance!

What an amazing sight to behold, as I watched Joy, pirouette, tap, and spin, and lay his soft shoes down so gently upon the ground. Immediately, Peace joined in and began to play his fiddle, and Love began to sing along.

The spectacle was so joyful and delightful to watch and hear that I just couldn't help but to get up and join in the dance, to move myself to the rhythm of the beat, to hop, boogie, and prance.

Peace played his fiddle, and Love sang along, while Joy and I danced to the delightful song. We danced and played the night away, right up to the early morning dawn. Then, afterwards, the four of us sat together and watched the sun rise. It was the most amazing and beautiful sight I've ever beheld, since I opened up and let Peace, Love, and Joy into my life!

The next day, I heard a knock at my door. I answered it. It was someone named, Get-Me-Down. He said: "I'm a traveler passing through, looking for a place to crash."

In response, I said to him, before I closed the door: "No Vacancy Here!" Finally, at last!

Story 3

OLD MAN ZUCKERMAN

AND

HIS NOISY OLE CANE

He walks with an itty-bitty gimp, a hitch, and a giddy up too; wielding a cane is his hand, with a mighty firm grip; dressed in a faded, tattered suit, and scuffed up, bent over shoes; sportin a dusty, secondhand, Stetson hat, with a cocked down brim; movin like a snail, as he slowly inches himself along, down a long, city sidewalk street, while he whistles to the tune of his favorite song.

A rap, a tap, tap… a rap, a tap, tap… goes his noisy ole cane, as he gingerly passes by; whistling that all so familiar refrain off key. Suddenly, he stops and pauses, but, only for a moment, to wipe his sweaty brow, with a dingy, white, monogram handkerchief that bears a stranger's mark. Then, he continues on his way, without notably missing a beat… a rap, a tap, tap… a rap, a tap, tap… goes his noisy ole cane, as it forcefully strikes hard against the ground, while he whistles to the sound of the beat.

Old man, Zuckerman, is his name; the man from Okoboji, with his noisy ole cane. A rap, a tap, tap… a rap, a tap, tap… goes that annoying, disturbing, and irritating sound — like the blasts of a jackhammer worker pounding on the street, or a big ole woodpecker steadily drumming on a tree!

A rap, a tap, tap... a rap, a tap, tap… "Here he comes! Here comes old man, Zuckerman! He's right on time today; the same as all other previous days!" many curious onlookers confirm and say. "Day after day, like clockwork, he passes by our way, along this same ole path, no later than ten o eight. Strolling pass the barbershop… pass the hardware store… and then, finally, down and around the corner drugstore at the end of the street. He's traveled this way for so long a time that he's even worn a path in the cement! A rap, a tap, tap… a rap, a tap, tap… goes the sound of his noisy ole cane, as it forcefully strikes hard against the ground, while he whistles to the tune of his favorite song, with an occasional shrill, shriek, and squeal! Old man, Zuckerman is his name, the man from Okoboji, with his noisy ole cane!" A rap, a tap, tap… a rap, a tap, tap!

He has no special skills or hidden talents; no good looks; no higher education. He's got little credit to his name, and even less cash. He's just an ordinary, everyday guy, with worn out knees and spindly legs; sportin a crooked smile, with two spaced teeth in the middle, wide enough to place three stacked quarters between.

He's sure to stir up a giggle, illicit a smile, or inspire a joke or two, from onlookers, as they watch him pass through. For he walks with an itty-bitty gimp, a hitch, and a giddy up too; wielding a cane is his hand, with a mighty firm grip; dressed in a faded, tattered suit, and scuffed up, bent over shoes; sportin a dusty, secondhand, Stetson hat, with a cocked down brim; movin like a snail, as he slowly inches himself along, down a long, city sidewalk street, while he whistles to the tune of his favorite song.

A rap, a tap, tap… a rap, a tap, tap… goes the sound of the cane.

"Look at old man, Zuckerman," people stop, and look, and say. "Every single day, he passes along our way; no later than ten o eight. Strolling pass the barbershop… pass the hardware store… and then, finally, down and around the corner drugstore at the end of the street. He's traveled this way for so long a time that he's even worn a path in the cement! A rap, a tap, tap… a rap, a tap, tap… goes his annoying cane! The sound of it is almost enough to drive you to go insane!"

As the people and curious onlookers chatter amongst themselves, about old man, Zuckerman, and his noisy ole cane, he eventually reaches the end of the block. And then, he turns the corner, and disappears from sight. Afterwards, daylight gradually falls, and it turns to night.

~

It is now the next day, for yesterday has come and gone. The time is ten after ten in the morning. So one man at the Barbershop turns to those present, and he says: "It is now ten minutes after ten, according to my watch. Has anyone seen old man, Zuckerman? I wonder what's keeping him today, and why he's so late! Like clockwork, he always walks along this street, at the same time, each and every day, with his noisy ole cane."

"Oh, haven't you heard," the Barber sadly replies. "He died last night and went to heaven. I have to admit, the street's feeling a little empty and quiet, and the sky's a little blue, without old man, Zuckerman, and his noisy ole cane strollin through, with a rap, a tap, tap… a rap, a tap, tap… And him joyfully whistling along to his favorite tune!"

"We have to agree," the inquiring man, and all the other people present reply to the Barber. And then, continuing, with one harmonious voice they all say: "This Street will never ever be quite the same, from this day forward on, now that Old Man, Zuckerman, and his Noisy Ole Cane are gone!

Story 4

THE PIT OF DOOM

"Help…! Help…! Help…! Somebody help me! Help…! Help…! I've fallin into a trap! Please help me! Please!" I yelled and cried out loud, as I sat there, waist deep, suspended upright in the deadly pit of doom.

"Help me…! Help me…! I've fallen in quicksand, and I can't get out! Help…! Help…! Help…!" I continued to yell and frantically shout about.

Pausing for a moment, I stopped to listen, to see if someone heard my cries for help, who perhaps could come and rescue me. But, sad to say, no one was there. No one was around to hear my pleas, as I lied there helplessly, slowly sinking into the ground.

~

Narrator:

Poor, Everest Hothmyer! Never in his wildest dreams would

he had ever imagined to be in this frightening mess and gloom; sitting in a deadly pool of earth, water, and sand — the colloid of liquefied soil — the thirsty swallower and hungry destroyer of souls, that lies quietly, secretly, and patiently in wait for the unwary to blindly happen upon and fall into its trap; this unimaginable fate and nightmare in the horrifying *"Pit of Doom!"*

~

Everest Hothmyer:

Angry and upset, I thought to myself: *"How could I let this happen? Why wasn't I alert to the possible dangers that might lie hidden in my path? Why did I allow myself to fall into the horrible and sad situation of this death dealing trap? Dropping… sinking… descending… slowly plummeting downward into the pit of misery and despair — the large, highly inescapable, deadly pothole that in one huge, big gulp, can swallow a man whole!"*

~

Narrator:

Unfortunately, the crazy; but, yet, scientifically truthful thing about quicksand, is that the more that a person wiggles, squirms or moves, or tries to fight it, the faster they sink.

Initially, when Mr. Hothmyer first stepped into the pit, he was knee deep in quicksand. But, then, he slowly and gradually began to sink up to his waist, where he now unfortunately stands.

Frantically searching and looking for a way out, Everest proceeds to quickly assess the situation and scan the area for something that he can perhaps reach, something that possibly can be used to help pull him up and out of the open pit. However, sad to say, to his misfortune and daunting dismay, he finds absolutely nothing, not a single thing that might help to save him from this overwhelming frightful situation and state— this most awful and horrifying fate! All he can do now is to wait, hope, and see if someone who might be traveling nearby will happen to come his way before it's too late!

~

Everest Hothmyer:

I'm slowing sinking, dropping, descending further and deeper into the bottomless pit of despair — the cold, callus, insensitive, heartless and cruel, death dealing chasm — the camouflaged, open grave, that secretly lays its trap for the unexpected and unwary victim to step into. I can't help but to panic and scream, knowing that this horrible predicament that I've gotten myself into, for a certainty, spells my ultimate doom!

Help me...! Help me...! Help...! Help...! Help...!" once again I proceed to scream at the top of my lungs. But, sadly, to no avail. For there is no one anywhere around to pull me up and out of this incarcerating pit of doom, this tormenting place of hell!

"This is crazy!" I screamed with a loud and angry voice.

"Man... I'm dumb! I'm nothing but a big, stupid idiot! How in the world could I have let this happen; to fall into this awful mess?" Everest angrily says to himself, with a lump in his throat, a whimper in his voice, and tears in his eyes, as he finally breaks down and starts to weep, with a painful cry.

~

Narrator:

Unfortunately, with the passing of time, with the ticking away of each and every moment on the clock, Everest proceeds to slowly descend further into the pit of agony and despair. For he is now up to his chest in quicksand.

As he lies there contemplating the truth and inevitability of his extremely bad situation and plight, he begins to panic even more! Then, suddenly, his whole life begins to quickly flash before his eyes.

Moving at the speed of light, Everest's mind begins quickly thumbing through every page in the extensive library of books that are conveniently stored and tucked away in the small compartments, crevices, and recesses of his extremely complex, human mind.

The truth is, because the pangs of death has no censure or off switch; at a time that you do not wish or want it to, it will blurt out any and everything about you, concerning things that have happened in your entire life, even things that you may not have been fully aware or conscience of in the past; or about the things that you deliberately tried to hide and bury away in the back of your mind — things that you are perhaps ashamed of, or that you are too cowardly to accept and face. The reason why is because death holds no secrets; it tells no lies. It is a revealer of secrets. It leaves nothing uncovered and unspoken, no stone unturned. It reveals all and everything about you (from your idiosyncrasies, down to your tiniest of faults), any and everything that you may have willfully or unconsciously put or stashed away deep into your psyche or locked deep within the chambers and vaults of your mind and brain. Interestingly, during this amazing unveiling process, people often view or see life in a completely different and much clearer way than they ever did in the past. However, unfortunately, it is also a time when extreme guilt and shame can surface to plague your mind, heart, and soul, about the things that you should have done or tried, or even failed to do, when you had the opportunity and time (while you were still alive).

~

Everest Hothmyer:

Suddenly, my whole life began to flash before my eyes. It candidly told me the complete truth about times of distant past.

It reminded me about everything: about the things I've seen; and places I've been; and also about the things I've done; failed to do; and the things that I've said.

"I should have hugged my mom and dad, and told them how much I love them. I should've gone out to lunch with my sister, or for a cup of coffee or tea. I should have found and married the girl of my dreams, and settled down and had children, a nice family. I should have traveled and seen the *Seven Wonders of the World*: (1) the "Great Pyramid of Giza," (2) the "Great Wall of China," (3) "Petra," (4) the "Coliseum in Rome," (5) "Chichen Itza," (6) "Machu Picchu," and (7) the "Taj Mahal." I should have learned to play a musical instrument. And, I should've written a book. I should have done something special, good, and important to be remembered for; to leave behind my indelible mark for doing something to make a difference in the world or in someone's life, instead of foolishly squandering and wasting my time away, from year to year, and from day to day. Now, here I am, about to die this shameful and humiliating death in a stupid hole; sinking into oblivion, disappearing forever from sight, into the depths of darkness, within the cold and lifeless bowels of the earth; an incredibly sad and miserable fate that no one on earth deserves to suffer and die. Never in my wildest imagination would I have ever thought that the earth would open its mouth and swallow me alive!

~

Narrator:

As time progresses, Everest sinks further and deeper into the pit of doom. He is now up to his neck in quicksand. It is just below his Adams apple.

~

Everest Hothmyer:

Suddenly, as I looked up and into the far distance; beyond

natures natural door or opening—a gap in the trees (a wide-open doorway that's located within the tall trees that outline the dense woodland and forest, that forms both a gateway entryway into the woods, and also an exit that leads to a spacious, open clearing—a grassy field of overgrown blades), I happened to spot and see the image of a person, who appears to be in the shape of a woman, with long, flowing, golden hair.

"Wait a minute," I thought to myself, as I zoomed in and closely focused in on the image: *"Is that my friend, Joy Willabee? Could it be that she came to look for and find me, as she has so often done in the past? Especially, during highly difficult and stressful times, when I'm feeling ever so down and blue; when things are just not going well; during times when I need to get away for a while, to try to make rhyme and sense out of it all?"*

"Joy…! Joy…! I'm over here! Joy…! Joy…! It's me, Everest! Help me…! Help me…! Help me, Joy!" I shouted as loud as I could.

In response, Joy turned and looked at me; but, in a way as though she didn't hear, or even care. And then, she turned away, and quickly vanished into thin air.

With tears in my eyes, and a whimper in my voice, I yelled: "Joy, come back! Joy, please come and rescue me! Come and lend me your helping hand! Come and pull me up and out of this death dealing mixture of water and sand. So I can once again stand upon solid ground; the place where I used to walk; the happy place where I use to reside, on the clouds of heaven, to where the sun reaches out and greets the sky! Can't you see that I'm lying here in trouble, distress, sadness, and pain? Help me!" I yelled at the top of my voice. "Help me, Joy! Oh, Joy, please hear my cries for help! Come and save me from this awful predicament and horrible mess that I've gotten myself into—this miserable fate of impending doom!"

~

Narrator:

The quicksand has now reached up higher—all the way up to Everest's mouth. He is trying his hardest to keep it up and out of the pit. But, unfortunately, he is fighting a losing battle. Finally, after taking his last breath of fresh air, his mouth falls beneath the surface, and then his eyes.

With his head now fully submersed beneath the surface, in sheer desperation, Everest proceeds to raise his hands up and out of the quicksand towards the sky. And then, all of the sudden, he feels a strong hand clasp around and tug on his wrist. Then he feels his body start to rise. It rises up and up, until it is completely out of the pit. And it keeps on climbing and ascending, way up high, clear over darkened clouds, and the bluest of skies; straight on up to the happy place, to where the sun greets the sky!

~

As soon as Everest reaches the destination above, a place called *"The Resplendent City of Silver, Pearls, and Gold,"*— to his surprise, he sees that Joy is there, standing by his side. However, for some reason, Joy has a much different appearance than she used to have in the past. For her face glows with a growing brightness, radiance, and splendor that Everest has never before seen; a brightness of true effervescence beauty that could never be surpassed!

~

Everest Hothmyer:

"Joy, you did it! You came to my rescue and aid after all; at both a time and in way that I would never have imagined. You saved me once again! Thank you, for your help, and for being my friend!"

In response, Joy says: "Overwhelmly sadness is like being in quicksand. It can consume and swallow a person whole. It can sink them into the pit of misery and despair, and even take away their life and soul. You see, in life there are many uncertainties. You never know what tomorrow will bring. One day, you can be on top of the world. And then, the next day, you can fall into a dark hole or pit. When that happens, the best advice is to get back up, and never, ever quit!"

In happy reply, Everest says to Joy: "Luckily, I have nothing to fear anymore. For nothing can get and pull me down again into the depths of darkness, despair, and gloom, that lay deep beneath the surface, where true pain and misery lie. Because, I am determined to never again leave your loving, upbuilding, and most encouraging side! For Joy, has the strength needed to keep me upon solid and stable ground, and the power to pull me up and out of anything, even the very scary, seemingly insurmountable and overwhelming 'Pit of Doom!'"

NOTE TO READER

This book is fiction. Any reference to historical events, real people or places are used fictitiously. Other names, characters, places, and events are products of the author's imagination, and any resemblance to actual events or places or persons, living or dead, is entirely coincidental.